Monsters and Ghosts

By C. J. Henning

Other books available on Amazon.com, Booksamillion and Barnes and Noble. Some available on Kindle.

FICTION:

Saga of Everstream: Tiathan Eiula And The War of The Seven Fortresses Vol. 1 & 2.

Whirliwind Sage And The Arbushi Wars.

Wormwood

On The Morning Of The First Day

The Last Messiah

COMMENTARIES:

Common Sense or Who Is That Sitting In My Pew?

Common Sense, Too or Are You Still Sitting In My Pew?

I Will Not Apologize For Christ

CHILDREN'S BOOKS

John Taddleboch And The Weegie Worts

Nursery Rhyme and Fairy Tale Mysteries

More Mysteries of Nursery Rhymes And Fairy Tales

Tittle Tattle Tales

A Walk In the Dark

POETRY:

Complete Poetry 1968-2000

Cathedral

Nonsense Rhymes

More Nonsense Rhymes

Even More Nonsense Rhymes

Risen and Rising

Random Thoughts Of An Old Man

Thinking of Love

Love Abounds

Patriot Dreams and Dreams of God

Whispering Sweet Nothings

Death And Other Party Favors

Visions of Love

PLAYS:

The Plays Vol 1 & 2

The Beastie

This is a true account of what I believe is a close encounter of a creature long lost in the deep woods that surrounds the cabin I just purchased. I almost never accept tales of strange creatures roaming the area. This one is called the "Beastie" that had forced the disappearance of past owners of this place.

I believe it's some local teens that don't like outsiders staking a claim on their land. I refuse to allow anyone to force me off this land. Still, I won't travel at night through the forest behind me though it is a short cut to the town below.

However, I enjoy the peace and quiet that I could not find in the city I left for the seclusion of the mountains. It did not take long for the locals to tell me of the legend of a creature, called the "Beastie", that has chased away anyone who lived in my cabin. One or two disappeared in the last two years presumably killed and buried far in the deep woods.

My first night was uneventful though I let my imagination run away with me a little. I thought I heard a low moan from the back of my cabin. When I looked, I found it was gas water heater behind the bathroom walls.

The second night was different. In the middle of the night, I could swear I heard a scratching on the outside walls. I took a flashlight with me and searched outside finding what I thought were scratch marks on my outside wall.

It could have been any animal and not the "Beastie" the locals keep telling me about. So I installed outside security lights with motion detectors which have helped a little.

What unnerved me a week later was the rustling of branches and bushes just out of view of the security lights. I took a flashlight with me as I investigated the noise thinking the locals were playing a prank. I took a baseball bat with me just in case.

Searching for an hour I only heard crickets and croaking frogs from the nearby pond. I could only go back to my cabin giving the locals the first win at trying to scare me. They could be as dangerous as the so-called "Beastie".

The following account still chills me to the bone and I have no answer to the event. The sun was setting when I realized I had not gotten groceries for Sandy's Food Mart. All I had left was a few pieces of bread and peanut butter.

I put on my jacket and ventured into the woods hoping I would get into town before dark. I was not afraid of the "beastie", but the locals did concern me. My trip down the mountain was uneventful and quiet. After I bought a few things I started the long trek up the road around the forest. The moon was half bright and I figured it would take about an hour to get home.

It was only a short walk when I heard a couple of

townies calling me from behind. I looked back to see three men with canes and a hammer pointing at me. My instinct was to run into the forest and lose them. If they believed the legend they wouldn't follow.

I was wrong. While heading up the mountain I heard them laughing and calling my name. I zigzagged off the trail to keep ahead of them. It was then I heard a different sound in front of me. A chill ran down my spine wondering how they could have gotten ahead of me.

My hand began to shake because I had nothing to defend myself with. The thrashing to my right came close, but passed me by. Thinking they missed me, I dashed quickly towards my cabin. It was then I heard the screaming, loud piercing cries for help for God or anyone else to stop the pain.

Then there was silence. A low moan crept up the mountain that spurred me onward. Footsteps paced themselves with each one of mine. I had already dropped my groceries and ran full tilt to my cabin door. Slamming it shut, I listened for anything that might have followed me.

Long ponderous footsteps came up to my door as I locked and chained myself in. Heavy breathing seemed to move the door in and out slightly. I found it hard to breathe not knowing where to hide. Did this thing outside kill the three men following me or was it part of elaborate plot to force me to leave the mountain?

The heavy breathing came close to my door where I could clearly hear and feel its presence. Then only one word could I hear. It said "Soon." After that the heavy footsteps left my porch and back into the woods.

Needless to say, whether locals or "Beastie" I went back to the city and never came back to the cabin. I didn't even ask about the three men though there were State Police parked outside the forest when I left.

One other thing, on my porch the next morning I

found a hammer and two canes with blood on them. Whether it was some strange creature or a hermit who thought he owned the forest, I never found out. Nor will I ever try.

The Cave

Ben and Jim were two avid hikers walking over the Bay Bridge Mountains though they were told to stay out of the many caves that could be found where they were traveling. The warning was for their own safety since most of the caves were long and deep with various offshoots that could get the best traveler lost.

Some of the mountain folk told stories of small ogre-like men who inhabited these caves and did not like visitors. Ben and Jim laughed at these legendary folk and figured they were only people who wanted to be left alone.

Ben was more cautious than Jim hoping not to run into anyone on the paths including bears or cougars. Ben kept a hunting knife with him always and Jim was partial to the bow and arrow which tended to be cumbersome when climbing up hillsides.

The first day was a cool 52o and cloudy which is what the weather report said on their battery radio. Jim shot a rabbit and fixed it for dinner which helped them use less of their supplies. Water was abundant every couple of miles as they watched waterfalls cascade down the mountains.

The first night was a little different as they camped near one of the numerous caves. Ben swore he saw someone watching them from the rocks across the clearing where they settled. Jim saw nothing and told Ben to sleep it off.

The second day had them far from civilization with grand views of the lakes and forest beneath them. Jim motioned to Ben to come near the precipice where he stood. Pointing beneath them, he asked Ben what he saw.

Ben looked at a small band of men

wandering towards a cave at the end of one of the lakes. A chill went down his spine as one of the small men pointed towards them causing the others to run inside the cave.

Jim wanted to go down and investigate, but Ben wanted to leave them alone. Jim wanted to know if these were the ogres the local townspeople had believed lived in the caves. Ben wanted to continue on their trip.

That night, Jim harassed Ben about searching the caves to see who these people were. Ben wanted to just sleep. The next morning, Ben found Jim had left with his bow and arrow. Upset, he set off to find Jim whom he believed would get himself in trouble. If these were mountain people, unlikely ogres, Ben thought they would not like to be disturbed.

At the first cave he found, Ben called out Jim's name without an answer. Taking a few steps in, he looked around seeing cobwebs and mold that had not been disturbed for years.

At the second cave, he found rocks and branches strewn over the cave floor. Someone had been inside so he called out Jim's name. An echo is all that answered him. A second call brought the same. Ben entered further inside to see if anything would tell him where his friend might be.

As he turned to leave, Ben heard a crack under his foot and looked down. The shaft of an arrow lay beneath him. Whether it was Jim's or not, he couldn't tell.

There were two shafts that led downward, but he needed his flashlight to investigate. He called Jim's name one last time before going back to their camp.

When he arrived at the campsite, Ben found all their gear strewn everywhere. His heart started to pound knowing something must have happened to Jim. Could it have been the small men they saw yesterday? Anyway, he found his flashlight near a pile of rocks and picked it up.

Walking back to the cave, Ben took out his hunting knife before going in. He made sure he never lost sight of the entrance because he was sure he would get lost otherwise.

His heart pounding as he heard voices far ahead and ventured toward the sound in case it was Jim's. As he got closer, a glimmer of light allowed him to turn off his flashlight.

Turning a corner, Ben saw a small group of disfigured men around a fire. They were standing over someone who was lying on the ground. The one on the ground was as small as they were, but moaning in pain.

Ben crept closer to see what was going on. When he got near enough, he looked down at the one the others were mumbling over. Squinting hard, Ben searched the face that seemed familiar, but disfigured like the rest of them.

Whatever it was, the thing looked up at him and cried out "Ben!" Ben shook convulsively at the sight of his friend who now looked like the rest of the creatures that surrounded him. "Run!" Jim cried out.

Ben turned and ran as he heard footsteps following him when he reached the entrance of the cave. The only path he could find was back down the mountain. When he entered the town that he and Jim left, Ben collapsed in front of an old woman.

Ben looked up pleading for help. She looked down and told him that no one could help him now. "You're one of them now." She held up a mirror so that Ben could see himself with a misshapen face and stubby gnarled hands. As he rose up he found himself half her height.

The old woman pointed towards the mountain and said "Off you go, now. They're waiting for you."

Legend of Lake Mickabob

It was the beginning of Fall when young newlyweds Andre and Mary Wentworth came to Lake Mickabob. Their honeymoon was at a rented cabin looking over the lake and the mountains beyond.

As the newlyweds started to unpack their luggage, two locals walked up to them. They were both in their fifties and seemed to be friendly.

"Welcome to Lake Mickabob. I'm George." George offered his hand.

"And I'm Henry." The other local waved their way.

"I'm Andre and this is my wife, Mary."

Andre shook George's hand. "Can I help you?"

"No, we thought we would let you know about the lake." Henry looked serious.

"What about the lake?" Andre became suspicious that these men were not there to welcome them.

"I think you should know that it would be best you didn't go on the lake at night." George pointed toward the open water.

"Why not?" Mary sighed just a little.

"You haven't heard about the legend?" Henry looked surprised.

"What legend?" Andre had little time to hear ghost stories from the locals who probably didn't want them there.

"There's a mysterious creature that roams the waters soon after dark." George began the tale. "First a batch of thick fog begins to float over the lake before the creature appears."

"You're kidding." Mary almost laughed.

"It's true!" Henry looked indignant.

"Well, thanks for the warning." Andre turned to take their suitcases into the cabin.

"You take care now." George shrugged his shoulders and started back down the path leading to town.

"Mind what we said." Henry followed him.

"Do you believe that?" Mary looked at Andre and laughed. "The nuts didn't fall from the tree."

"I saw a couple of boats at the pier." Andre nodded toward the lake. "And there's a full moon tonight. If we're lucky we might catch a glimpse of this creature."

"Should we bring something to protect ourselves?" Mary wondered with a smile.

"Maybe extra chips." Andre frowned.

As the sun set, Andre and Mary started a fire in the fireplace to keep the evening chill from overwhelming the cabin. Then they walked hand in hand towards the lake. Mary got in the boat first then Andre pushed it away from the pier before rowing to the center of the lake.

"I wonder when the monster will make it's appearance." Mary looked around the lake that had a sunset glow to it.

"There's no fog, so we are safe." Andre laughed as each stroke pulled them further from the pier.

"I'm glad we got away from the family." Mary enjoyed the peace and quiet listening to the crickets and croaking of frogs.

"The moon is beginning to rise." Andre stopped rowing and sat next to Mary.

"Careful, we might tip over." Mary helped him next to her.

As darkness enveloped the lake, Andre and

Mary did not see the mist coming from the far shore. They looked up at the stars as the boat drifted further away. It was Mary who first saw the fog coming towards them.

"What do you think?" Mary pointed to the thick mass coming towards them.

"Only our imagination." Andre kissed her cheek.

"Let's go in just in case." Mary's pulse quickened.

"It's nothing." Andre tried to reassure her.

"We won't see the moon if it gets any closer." Mary pushed him toward the oars.

Reluctantly, Andre slowly rowed toward the pier. A low moan shook him as he stared at the moving fog. Mary urged him on. Before they reached the pier something very large hit their boat tossing them into the water.

"Swim!" Andre urged Mary to the shore.

When they reached the shore, Andre grabbed Mary's hand as they ran toward the cabin. Something huge was coming out of the water and following them. The ponderous steps shook the ground beneath them as they slammed the cabin door behind.

"What do we do?" Mary looked to Andre who pulled her to the bedroom which was the furthest from the front door. Andre was sure they could not outrun the thing outside the cabin.

Whatever it was stopped just outside the cabin letting out a painful moan. Andre and Mary held their breath until the cabin shook from some unknown monster that wanted to get inside.

Just as suddenly, whatever it was, turned and went back into the lake. Andre waited an hour before venturing outside. He saw deep footprints leading to and from the cabin. The north wall was damaged from whatever tried to get in.

"It's gone." Andre told Mary.

"What do we do?" Mary still shook.

"We pack and leave in the morning." Andre did not care what it was, but leaving was the only answer.

In the morning, Andre and Mary were met by George and Henry. They didn't seem to be surprised at what Andre and Mary told them.

"Whatever it was." Andre explained. "It's huge and dangerous."

"We told you not to go on the lake at night." George tried to be consoling.

"Can we help you?" Henry saw Mary struggling with her suitcase.

"No, thanks." Mary closed the car door as they quickly left George and Henry behind.

"What's up, guys?" Another local came up to them.

"Harry! You outdid yourself!" George patted him on the back.

"What are you talking about?" Harry was perplexed.

"One thing though." Henry pointed to the ground. "How did you get these footprints done so quickly?"

"Footprints?" Harry shook his head.

"You scared the heck out of those newlyweds." George began to wonder what was wrong with Harry.

"I don't know what you're talking about." Harry stared at the ground and then looked at the damaged cabin. "What happened here?"

"Did you use your tractor to do this?" Henry saw the troubled look on Harry's face. "It's going to take a while to fix it."

"I didn't do this." Harry insisted.

"We've been doing this for ten years and now you say you didn't do this?" George was concerned now.

"My wife was sick last night so I thought I would do it tonight instead." Harry looked over at the lake.

"Then what was…." George was confused.

"You don't think…" Henry shook his head.

"I tell you guys I'm not lying." Harry insisted as the three of them walked towards town as a thick fog followed them.

The Thing Under Carriage Bridge

Tentatively, four children, each twelve years old, crept towards Carriage Bridge as the sun began to set. Their leader of the group was Jeremy followed by Will, Johnny and Bill who did not look like they wanted to be there. They heard from Jeremy that there was a thing, a monster that hid under the bridge at night which did not like to be disturbed.

"I don't want to get any closer." Will was the first to speak up.

"Chicken!" Jeremy had a hard time getting them together just to reach the bridge.

"Tell us again about what is under this bridge." Johnny shook slightly not liking to be out at night anyway.

"I heard my father say that there is something living under the bridge that keeps everyone away." Jeremy enjoyed telling the story again to see them all shiver though it was a warm summer night. "I don't believe him so we need to find out if it's true."

"Then why don't you go in." Bill looked up at Jeremy hoping it wouldn't be himself.

"I already have." Jeremy puffed up his chest though he knew he was lying.

"When?" Bill wanted to know.

"Two weeks ago." Jeremy did not exactly lie since he did look under the bridge one bright afternoon.

"Really?" Johnny chimed up.

"So, who's going in now?" Jeremy searched each face. He saw the panic and fear on all of them.

"Not me" Bill stepped back.

"Or me." Will crossed his arms in defiance.

"Johnny?" Jeremy patted him on the back.

"I'm scared." Johnny stood frozen in place.

"So, you're yellow." Jeremy sensed that he could convince Johnny to go in. If he could convince the other two to pick on Johnny, he could get a real laugh.

"Yes." Johnny looked into the deep darkness with dread.

"Your saying you're chicken?" Bill saw the opportunity to push Johnny under the bridge.

"Don't make me do it." Johnny almost cried.

"You can't be one of us then." Jeremy knew he would convince Johnny to do what he asked.

"But I want to be...." Johnny was torn between his fear and the need for friendship. As it was, Johnny had only these three as friends.

"Then you need to do this to prove yourself." Jeremy insisted.

"Yeah, do it, Johnny." Will and Bill chimed up together themselves relieved Jeremy wasn't picking on them.

"If I call you for help, will you come?" Johnny asked with sad pleading eyes.

"Sure, we will." Jeremy thought to himself there was no way he would go in there.

Carriage Bridge overlooked a dry bed of trash and weeds that could be clearly seen in the daytime. At night there was no way to know what was there. Stray cats and dogs wandered the area looking for food. Jeremy thought Johnny would get a good scare and then run back to them.

"Okay." Johnny didn't want to lose his friends and began to venture into the yawning darkness. A strange odor like a soft wind passed between them. Jeremy thought he heard a low moan, but as he leaned closer the silence was deafening.

The three left behind waited a long time after Johnny disappeared beneath the bridge. They heard no cries for help, no footsteps or anything to let them know Johnny was all right.

"Johnny?" Will was the first one call to him.

No answer.

"Johnny!" Bill started to panic, but not go after his friend.

"He's tricking us." Jeremy hoped he was right.

"We can't leave him." Bill tried to urge them closer.

"Johnny!" Jeremy became impatient.

No answer.

"We have to tell someone!" Will began to panic.

"Our parents will punish us if we do." Jeremy fought the urge to run home.

"We need a flashlight." Will was already running

home. "You guys wait there!"

When Will came back, he shined the light under the bridge finding nothing but trash and weeds.

"Where did he go?" Bill wondered out loud.

"I bet he ran home." Jeremy thought of the only explanation.

"I bet he did, too." Will hoped it was true.

"Let's go home, too." Bill already started down the street.

The next day, there were adults and police searching for Johnny who never came home. They looked all day finding nothing. Jeremy, Will and Bill said nothing knowing no one would believe what really happened.

That night, Jeremy ventured back to the bridge hoping to find Johnny sitting on top. As he came closer, he thought he heard something in the dark beneath the bridge. He wasn't sure what he heard.

"Johnny?" Jeremy was hopeful that the rustling he heard was his friend. "Johnny? I'm sorry."

"Jeremy?" It was clearly Johnny's voice.

"Johnny come out of there." Jeremy was relieved to hear his voice. "Come out of there."

"Jeremy? Help me." Jeremy was sure it was Johnny.

"I'm coming." Jeremy ventured into the darkness.

"Hello, Jeremy." A gruff deep voice greeted him and swallowed up the scream when Jeremy cried out.

Shadows

Stan, the town drunk, staggered slowly to his makeshift home of a blanket and cardboard. If he wasn't a relative of the mayor, who disavowed him, the police would have thrown him past the town limits. This night was going to be a different night for Stan as watched passersby give him dirty looks.

Some kids taunted him about his dirty clothes and the stench coming from his abode. Stan took it in stride just so they didn't try to hurt him. All but one of the kids left him alone who was the oldest just turning sixteen. Stan knew him as Al, but that was all he knew of him. Al was a bully who felt better about himself by picking on the weak and people like Stan.

"How long you going to stink up this town, ya

bum?" Al came right up to Stan who tried to ignore him.

Al kicked at the cardboard leaving a couple of holes to let the October wind to pass through. Stan thought it best to move down the street and hide in a nearby alley. Al followed him so Stan turned down a dark alley.

"You afraid of me?" Al hesitated before he stood looking down the alley.

Stan hurried out the other side knowing Al would easily be left behind. He heard Al's footsteps while mumbling something that Stan didn't hear. The footsteps abruptly stopped which halted Stan in his tracks. He didn't see Al come out or retreat back down the alley.

"He's waiting for me to come back." Stan told himself, but his curiosity controlled his decision to find out.

Stan walked slowly back to the alley and peeked around the corner finding Al gone. Confused, he walked the entire length of the dark alley till he came back where he entered. Al was nowhere to be seen.

Stan knew this bully wouldn't give up that easy so stayed awake most of the night watching out for him. He eventually fell asleep.

In the morning, he heard some of the kids who bothered him yesterday talking about Al, who seemed to have disappeared. His parents were looking for him and so were his friends. Eventually the police came by and asked Stan some questions.

"So, you saw this kid last night?" Officer Black was sure Stan was drunk and didn't see anything he could use.

"He came by and kicked my home until I ran down that alley over there." Stan pointed down the street.

"Then what?" Officer Black didn't bother writing anything down.

"He followed me for a while, then I guess gave up." Stan frowned a little trying to make sense of it all. "When I came back he was gone."

"Okay, Stan, thanks." Officer Black sighed as he walked away thinking he did his duty.

Stan settled in for the day except for a walk in the park where he met a man in a long grey coat. The man stared waiting for Stan to say something.

"Can I help you?" Stan never saw this man before and felt a little uneasy.

"I'm here to help you." The man neither offered his name nor his hand.

"How so?" Stan was a bit bemused by him.

"Protection." The man tilted his head slightly as appraising a pet dog or cat.

"Why?" Stan was interested.

"An experiment." The man started to turn to go.

"What a minute!" Stan tried to stop him.

"Tonight." Was all that the man told him.

"You can't tell me this and walk away." Stan

watched the man pass a grove of trees. He ran to catch up to him, but the man was gone.

All day Stan wondered what the man meant by protection. Who would try to harm him? What did the man know that he didn't? A nice bottle of spirits would help clear or cloud his mind. Whichever didn't matter.

Mr. Dawson walked his dog, a German shepherd, at sunset and every time would have his dog relieve himself on Stan's makeshift home.

"What's wrong with you, Dawson!" Stan was tired of being harassed by him and his dog.

"You don't like it, leave!" Mr. Dawson knew Stan was related to the mayor, but he thought he could eventually be able to drive Stan out of town.

"You're nothing, but a jerk!" Stan became nervous as Mr. Dawson started to unchain his dog.

"My dog needs some exercise." Mr. Dawson grinned.

Stan ran towards the dark alley and hoped to find a place to hide as the barking came closer as he neared the end of the alley. Then the barking stopped suddenly.

"Harry?" Mr. Dawson called out, but his dog didn't come back.

Mr. Dawson entered the dark alley hoping to find his dog safe. Stan waited on the other side until there was complete silence. Venturing into the darkness, Stan did not find Mr. Dawson or his dog. Confused, Stan went back to his home and lay down.

In the morning, Stan was awakened by Officer Black who shook the cardboard walls. Stan came out rubbing his eyes.

"Have you seen Mr. Dawson or his dog?" Officer Black could see Stan already had his liquid breakfast.

"He came by and let his dog mess with my shelter." Stan pointed to the damp spot on the corner of his home.

"Then what?" Officer Black knew he would have to drag it out of him.

"He set his dog on me into that alley." Stan tried hard to remember.

"Then what?" Officer Black was becoming impatient.

"When I got to the other end and turned around, they were gone." Stan shrugged his shoulders.

"Gone where?" Officer Black sighed.

"Beats me." Stan scratched his beard. "All I know is that he went away and left me alone."

"No help at all." Officer Black walked away.

That evening, Mrs. Dawson came to Stan with a cane and a furious look. Stan stepped back waiting for the barrage of questions. Mrs. Dawson hated Stan as much as her husband because it made the town look dirty.

"You did something to my husband!" Mrs.

Dawson approached him. "I'll beat it out of you if I have to!"

"I don't know what happened to your husband…" Stan suddenly thought that the tall man in the park had something to do with this. Whoever he leads down the alley disappears, protecting him.

"Yes, you do!" She raised her cane, but Stan easily avoided her. His next move was to get her into the dark alley.

Mrs. Dawson followed him swinging her cane back and forth. As Stan reached the other end of the alley, he looked back to find Mrs. Dawson nowhere to

be found. Now he thought he had some power through this alley. Anyone who threatens him seem to disappear if he can lure them into the shadows.

For the next few weeks, six other individuals who threatened Stan disappeared abruptly. No bodied were found, but the town feared to go out at night for fear of being kidnapped by some psycho. Stan smiled to himself since no one suspected him.

Stan got the idea he could make anyone disappear till one night, Officer Black wanted to move him away. Stan believed he can get rid of anyone right or wrong. He pushed Black away and ran down the alley.

"I only want you to be safe!" Black followed him into the alley. Black came out the other side, but Stan was gone.

When he looked back behind him a tall man in a long grey coat stood there. As he went to talk with him, a cat knocked over an empty bottle. As he looked up again, the tall man was gone.

Officer Black waited a couple of hours and then a few days, but Stan never returned. No one disappeared from then on which made Officer Black suspect, but unable to prove Stan might have had something to do with it.

The Arkolytes

When the first body was found, two hikers thought, whoever it was, had accidently burned themselves trying to make a campfire. When the rangers came, they concluded the same thing. Just some fool tried to use lighter fluid to jump start the weekend.

As the weeks progressed, other bodies were found burned beyond recognition. All four victims were lying near the lake which was popular with many hikers. There were no signs of violence except deep burns.

Within a week later, rangers set up camps at various sites to find out if it was an accident or someone torching hikers. They still believed it had to be accidental lighting of campfires from novice campers. The Rangers warned anyone they saw to take care lighting fires.

Two particular rangers, Alex and Ray, set up for the night near the lake. As Ray looked over the water, he saw clouds of fireflies hovering just above the surface. It almost lit up the area with its aura.

As they settled in, an old man in baggy pants and a checkered shirt walked up to them. His hair was very disheveled and beard seemed to stick out in different directions.

"How are you, sir?" Ray, a rookie ranger, welcomed the interruption. It was his fourth night without seeing anyone.

"I will be fine." The old man sat down by their fire. "I'm Samuel and you might be careful if you plan to spend the night here."

"Ray." Ray shook Samuel's hand though he didn't offer it.

"Alex." Alex nodded wondering what brought Samuel there. "Why careful?"

"You see that mass of fireflies over the lake?" Samuel pointed behind them.

"Yeah." Alex felt a warmth emanating from the lake.

"Those aren't fireflies, but Arkolytes." Samuel watched as Alex let out a big guffaw.

"Arkolytes?" Ray was confused as he stared at the thousands of fireflies.

"Yeah, they have a long history in this area." Samuel sighed realizing their disbelief. "Best not to tick them off… or me."

"As long as they stay over the lake, neither of us will have a problem." Alex thought Samuel was a lonely hermit who enjoyed telling everyone ghost stories.

"I do not like so many people coming by and leaving their trash behind." Samuel owned half the land around the lake and was not kind to hikers.

"We heard that a few hikers have disappeared over the years." Alex squinted at Samuel. "Did you have something to do with their disappearances?"

"I encouraged a few to stay off my land." Samuel had a wry smile on his face. Changing the subject, Samuel continued. "Have you heard of the history of the Arkolytes?"

"I would." Ray sat down next to Samuel.

Samuel took out a pipe and a pouch of tobacco. Alex would have told him not to smoke, but the recent rains made it safe.

"Sure." Alex agreed since it was better than the boredom of conversation with Ray.

"Each year at this time, the Arkolytes come here to do their mating ritual." Samuel took a good puff from his pipe and leaned back. "However, they tend to be rather aggressive when someone interferes with that ritual. Some fools who camp here swat them or spray poison."

"So you've heard about the bodies we've found around here?" Alex became suspicious.

"Yes, sir, I have." Samuel puffed on his pipe.

"And you're going to tell us these fireflies…" Ray stood up.

"Arkolytes." Samuel corrected him.

Okay, Arkolytes are responsible for their deaths?" Ray was more than skeptical though he did notice the cloud of Arkolytes flying closer.

"How else would you explain it?" Samuel tapped the burnt tobacco on a stone next to him.

"Carelessness!" Alex almost yelled at him.

Ray wanted to know more, but could see Alex had enough. There was a twinkle in Samuel's eye that disturbed him. Samuel made no sudden moves, but Ray and Alex felt threatened by his presence.

"Maybe. Maybe not." Samuel seemed upset that they did not believe him. He patted his pocket as if looking for another match which seemed to signal the Arkolytes closer.

"I don't like this." Ray saw the mass of lights circling closer.

"You don't believe me." Samuel put his pipe away. "But you will."

"I think it's time for you to leave." Alex reached over and helped Samuel up.

"You're making a mistake." Samuel struggled a little to stay.

"Alex, maybe we should let him stay." Ray grabbed Alex's arm.

"Let me go, Ray!" Alex pushed Samuel away.

"Now it's too late." Samuel was upset, but left down the path back to his home.

As Samuel slowly left their camp, he could hear Ray and Alex screaming for help before an eerie silence overcame the night.

A couple of rangers came up the trail to relieve Ray and Alex only to find two charred bodies near the lake.

Monster In The Attic

The Johnson's just moved into an old Victorian house and loved to see the burnished bannisters that led up to the second and third floors. A second stairway led to the attic which impressed them less.

Harold and Victoria dreamt of having to own an old house they could fix up themselves. They were astounded at the low price, but attributed it to the many repairs that had to be made.

A local legend helped in getting the sale. Supposedly, an elderly couple with their grandson were found in the attic dead. The old woman was hung from the rafters while the old man and grandson were butchered by some unknown assailant. Some locals believed the old woman killed the other two and then hung herself.

Harold was informed there was a curse on those who lived there. He was told four other owners left the house in terror after only a few months living there. Victoria ignored the stories and immediately started decorating the first floor.

Harold went room to room fixing the lighting and painting the walls. It took a couple of months, but the house seemed to live again. They made themselves comfortable.

It was near the end of their renovation as Victoria almost fell asleep when she thought she heard someone walking above their bedroom in the attic.

"Harold?" Victoria nudged him.

"What?" Harold rubbed his eyes.

"Do you hear that?" Victoria now sat up, but could not hear anything.

"Hear what?" Harold listened intently, but there was nothing to hear.

"Nothing, I guess." Victoria lay back and fell asleep.

The next day, Harold and Victoria celebrated the end of fixing their home. The day was a time of rest and enjoying what they did.

"What was that?" Victoria heard something drop from upstairs.

"I'll go look." Harold searched the second floor and then the third, but saw nothing out of place.

"Did you look in the attic?" Victoria asked Harold who gave her a "Why me?" look.

As Harold approached the attic door, he heard rustling a few feet from the entrance. Hesitating, he went back downstairs and picked up his hammer before going back upstairs.

"Is someone there?" Victoria was getting anxious.

"Well, something anyway." Harold hoped he was wrong. "Probably a squirrel."

"I hope so." Victoria stayed at the foot of the stairs ready to call for help if needed.

Harold slowly opened the attic door listening to the high-pitched creak of the hinges. Entering in, a cold breeze passed over him.

"Anything?" Victoria just wanted to hear his voice after she lost sight of him.

"Pretty cold up here and dark, too." Harold smelled something foul in the air.

"Leave it be." Victoria didn't care what he found so long as he locked the door before he came down to her.

"Nothing." Harold turned to lock the attic door and headed downstairs.

"I wish they didn't tell us of the murders." Victoria was aggravated with herself, too. Letting ghost stories get to her was childish.

It was eleven o'clock when they finally made it to bed, but Victoria was still wide awake. Harold fell asleep immediately. Victoria drifted in and out.

"What was that?" She shook Harold awake.

"What was what?" he sounded as annoyed as he really was. It was becoming a nightly ritual with Victoria hearing things.

"Footsteps….in the attic!" She whispered harshly, not liking his tone.

"This is the last time I go up there." Harold reached for his flashlight.

Victoria listened while Harold clomped up the stairs, opened the attic door and went in. The silence was deafening until a loud thump startled her.

"Harold! You all right?" Victoria got out of bed.

There was no answer which worried her. Victoria slowly made her way up the stairs seeing it mostly dark, but Harold's flashlight was on the floor.

"Honey?" Victoria tried to see through the darkness.

She heard a deep grunt which made her jump. Victoria picked up the flashlight and used it to search the attic. It was then she froze seeing some huge thing holding her husband's head in its hand.

Dropping the flashlight, Victoria ran out of the house screaming into the night. The next day neighbors found her disheveled and incoherent. When they asked what happened, all she could say over and over again: "Monster in the attic! Monster in the attic!"

When the police went to investigate they found Harold's body, but couldn't believe Victoria had anything to with it since Harold's head was ripped off his shoulders. No monster was found.

The Eagle's Nest

"You know Tommy, someday I will fly away and get away from school and my parents." Jenny told her best friend. She was only nine years old, but already not happy with life.

"That would be nice." Tommy was only half listening. He was used to hearing Jenny wanting to turn into a bird and fly away. "But where would you go?"

"To the mountains over there." Jenny pointed to the snow-covered mountains in the distance.

"What else would you do?" Tommy sighed waiting to hear the same answer over and over again.

"I would fly free forever." Jenny had no plan but to reach the clouds.

"What would you eat...worms?" Tommy believed that birds only ate worms.

"I would become an eagle and live in a nest like that one up there." She pointed to the eagle's nest just above them. "Eagles don't eat worms."

"If I became a bird I would miss French fries and hamburgers." Tommy had to be practical because he was already hungry.

Their walk home from school was always the same, but Tommy didn't mind since he walked with the cutest girl in his class.

"I'd rather be free from homework and my parents telling me to do homework and then go to bed." Jenny rambled on.

"How do you think you'll become a bird?" Tommy absently asked her.

"An eagle! I decided I want to be an eagle!" Jenny insisted as she turned Tommy to look at her.

"Okay! Okay! An eagle!" Tommy worried she might hit him.

"I know if I climb that tree and jump into that nest, I will become an eagle and fly away." Jenny stared up at the eagle's nest.

"You're goofy." Tommy shook his head and walked on.

"Am not!" Jenny stopped pouting her lips.

"No one can turn into an eagle." Tommy thought Jenny was crazy.

"I can and I will. So there!" Jenny started toward the tree.

"Where are you going?" Tommy watched Jenny touch the tree where the eagle's nest sat at the top.

"I'll show you." Jenny started to climb on the branches leading to the top.

"No, no! You'll fall, Jenny!" Tommy was too late

to stop her from climbing up.

"No, I won't. I'm going to fly!" Jenny felt euphoric as she slowly reached each branch bringing her closer to the nest.

"What if there's an eagle already there?" Tommy was afraid she would fall and he would get blamed for not stopping her.

"I'll say hello." Jenny stopped for a second to catch her breath.

"Come down, Jenny!" Tommy started to panic even more as she almost reached the nest. "You're my best friend! Don't go!"

"I have to." Jenny reached the nest and climbed in.

"Jenny!" Tommy looked around to see if anyone could help him, but the streets were empty.

As he looked up a giant eagle arose from the nest and looked down at him. Tommy knew that Jenny had to be hurt because eagles don't like strangers in their nests.

"Jenny!" Tommy cried thinking the eagle had hurt her.

The eagle hesitated before spreading it wings and let the wind pick it up into the sky. The eagle circled over Tommy's head before coming down towards him.

"No!" Tommy fell to the ground hoping the eagle would not hurt him.

The eagle landed a few feet from him, tilting its head one way then the other as if to tell him something. Tommy didn't move for a while until the eagle lifted itself into the sky and toward the far mountains.

"Jenny!" Tommy got the nerve to climb up the tree to see if Jenny was all right. He kept calling her name, but received no answer.

"Jenny!" Tommy reached the nest and looked in only to find it empty.

"Jenny?" Tommy looked out toward the mountains seeing the eagle become a small dot in the sky.

The Borbonn

"Why are we exploring caves at midnight?" Jonathan Wicks was confused at the timing. He'd rather be sleeping.

"The locals talked about a creature called the Borbonn that only roams these creepy caves after midnight." Andrew Jacobs insisted that they lose a night's sleep in order to be scared to death instead.

"Isn't the Borbonn just an ugly ogre?" Jonathan lifted one eyebrow to illustrate his skepticism. "Or some poor deformed hermit who wants to be alone?"

"Borbonn sounds more enticing." Andrew lifted his lantern at the opening of the cave.

"Shouldn't we be quiet?" Jonathan wanted to go back to bed, but didn't want Andrew to go alone.

"Please don't jump at every little noise you hear." Andrew knew it would be tough to keep his friend calm.

"Tell me again what we're looking for?" Jonathan had second and third thoughts about this adventure.

"It's a lone creature that roams around here only seen by other cave explorers." Andrew tried to explain.

"Anyone die?" Jonathan was concerned they wouldn't survive the night.

"No, no, no one has died….yet." Andrew enjoyed needling him. "It seems this thing is not too quick or smart. We should be safe."

"What happens if we run into it?" Jonathan prayed they wouldn't.

"I want to snap a picture of it." Andrew held up

an instamatic camera.

"Then we can go back to the motel?" Jonathan wanted to find a bed not a monster.

"Relax." Andrew entered the cave with his lantern.

"Won't it see the light and run away?" Jonathan hoped.

"I have night vision for both of us." Andrew turned off the lantern and gave Jonathan a pair of goggles.

"Wow, I can see pretty good." Jonathan recognized rock formations and two openings in front of them.

"We'll try this way first." Andrew took the first tunnel on his right and then turned to his friend. "Keep quiet."

"Sure thing." Jonathan stayed solidly behind his friend. If they met the Borbonn it would grab Andrew first and he had a chance to get away.

The dim light seemed to cast shadows on the walls which made Jonathan jumpy. Andrew walked ahead without hesitation.

"What's that?" Jonathan's heart rate soared when he heard some stones falling in front of them.

"Just some loose stones!" Andrew hissed quietly. "Relax!"

"We're going to get ourselves killed and he wants me to relax." Jonathan mumbled under his breath forcing Andrew to turn and stare at him into silence.

"You're being a baby, Jonathan." Andrew slapped Jonathan's shoulder.

"I'll be glad to cry for you." Jonathan was almost serious.

"Just an hour more. That's all I ask." Andrew continued on.

Neither said another word as they searched the

inner tunnels, but did not venture too far in case they needed to leave suddenly. An hour went by when Andrew sighed turning to his friend only to find an ugly monstrous face not three inches from his own.

Jonathan had already left him seeing the Bourbon first coming out of a tunnel nearby. Andrew shook with fear before stumbling past the creature dropping his lantern and camera.

"Where did you go?" Andrew met Jonathan outside the cave. "Why didn't you warn me?"

"It came out of nowhere next to me and I couldn't say anything." Jonathan was glad to see Andrew was safe.

"I almost had a heart attack." Andrew pulled Jonathan further away from the cave entrance.

"Did you get a picture?" Jonathan innocently asked.

"Sure! Go on back and get the camera." Andrew had no intention going back in.

"You saw it?" Jonathan wondered what it looked like. "I only saw something huge from the shadows."

"It was awesome!" Andrew calmed himself down realizing he had encountered the Borbonn and lived. "Ugly! Creepy!"

A noise made them jump as they thought they saw something move inside the cave. The sight only spurred their way back down the mountain to a couple of warm beds.

Jack o'Lantern

Sure, it was Halloween and everyone was in costume pilfering candy from all the neighbors. Later, playing practical jokes. It was expected. Billy and Larry decided to smash pumpkins as their form of fun entertainment.

Billy picked up a grinning pumpkin near the end of their street and smashed it on the ground. Running away they were laughing and pushing each other back and forth.

As they turned the corner, another pumpkin sat in the middle of the road, but this one had a snarling face etched on its front.

"That one is staring at you." Larry giggled pulling Billy towards it.

"It won't for very long." Billy picked it up and held it over his head. "Ow!"

"What's the matter?" Larry stopped laughing.

"If I didn't know better, I think it bit me." Billy saw a trickle of blood come from his thumb.

"Look at its face!" Larry was suddenly frightened.

"Why?" Billy held the jack o'lantern in front of him to see that it was now smiling at him. He dropped it on the road and they both ran off.

"It's just our imagination." Larry repeated over and over again.

"Yeah." Billy wanted to believe it.

They turned to go home and stopped suddenly seeing the jack o'lantern staring up at them on a grassy knoll.

"It's not real." Billy looked around. "Someone is messing with us."

"Come out you cowards and face us!" Larry agreed with Billy.

Silence except from some of the children on the next street. Billy looked up at the jack o'lantern and could swear it had turned toward him. The eyes seemed to glow though there were no candles inside it.

"We better get out of here." Larry turned back and there on the sidewalk was the jack o'lantern. Billy turned to see that the one on the grassy knoll had vanished.

"It can't be the same one." Billy tried to convince himself.

"Maybe it's mad because you tried to smash it." Larry thought it was a crazy idea even as he said it.

"It's not real." Billy kicked it aside.

They ran for blocks until they neared the park thinking it was safe since there was carnival in the middle. Still, they had to go through the woods to get to the brightly lit rides and food concessions.

"Wait!" Larry pulled Billy back as he saw the jack o'lantern leaning against a tree in front of them.

"This is too creepy." Billy refused to go near it.

"Someone is really seriously messing with us." Larry felt his skin crawl.

They looked away and then back again seeing that the jack o'lantern was no longer smiling, but frowning. Billy visibly shook with fear.

"I'm sorry." Billy tried to apologize to it.

"Come on." Larry pulled Billy out of the woods.

"What can we do now?" Billy wanted to go home and hide under his bed covers.

"Find some way to get home." Larry seemed to read his friend's mind.

They ran for blocks through neighbor's yards and alleyways to lose whoever was playing this elaborate joke on them. Just a block from their homes, they sighed a sigh of relief. The path seemed clear as they slowly walked home.

"Oh, no!" Larry saw the jack o'lantern on top of Billy's mailbox grinning at them both with fiery eyes.

They almost expected it to talk which is when they heard the hoofbeats. They knew no one owned horses except on a ranch far out of town.

"Do you hear that?" Billy looked down the street in the darkness.

"What is that?" Larry saw someone riding a black horse towards them.

"Can you see who it is?" Billy saw a cloaked figure with a hood that seemed to cover his face.

As the figure came closer, neither Billy nor Larry could see who the rider was, but he was riding straight at them.

"Get out of the way!" Larry pushed Billy to the ground as the rider leaned over and picked up the jack o'lantern placing it on his shoulders.

"Don't hurt us!" Larry pleaded as the grinning pumpkin looked down at them.

The mouth seemed to move, but nothing came out. The horse lifted its front legs as if to stomp them, but the rider turned it around and ran off. Billy and Larry thought they heard laughter and resolved not to tell anyone what happened. Who would believe them?

Cry In The Night

It was a moonless night as Jacob Sanders walked the two miles home. There was a forest that divided his house from the rest of the town. It seemed quieter than usual without crickets or other insect noises.

This is the umpteenth time he passed this way, usually with his wife, Helen, when they walked by the same site. They were married for thirty years until she died this day a year ago.

A deep sadness enveloped Jacob this night as he felt a great emptiness inside him as he walked. The silence suddenly was broken by the sad sound of someone crying just a few feet from the road.

"Hello?" Jacob hesitated for a moment.

The crying continued and Jacob could tell it was the voice of a woman. He cautiously entered the forest finding a woman sitting on a fallen tree with her back to him. She was wearing a cloak with a hood hiding her face.

"Are you all right?" Jacob stood behind her.

"I lost my husband." She held her face in her hands.

"I'm sorry." Jacob wondered why she was sitting in the middle of a forest. "Should you be here?"

"I just found myself here." She would not look at him.

"Did he die?" Jacob wanted to keep her talking.

"No, I left him." She cried again.

"Why?" Jacob wanted to comfort her, maybe hold her to show he cared.

"I had no choice." She wiped her face with a hankie.

"I lost my wife a year ago to cancer." Jacob

thought about that day. "We walked past this forest almost every night. Now I walk alone."

"I left my husband, but I didn't want to." She turned further away from him. "I'm sure he's missing me."

"Should I call him for you?" Jacob reached for his phone.

"No, it's no use." She started to weep again.

"Why did you leave?" Jacob sat next to her.

"It was my time." She bowed her head, the sorrow in her voice overwhelmed him.

"What does that mean?" Jacob did not understand. "Do you still love him?"

"I love him and miss him." She moved a little away from him. "We were inseparable."

"Then why?" Jacob had to know.

"I couldn't help it!" Her cry was almost a scream.

"Tell me more about him." He changed the

subject trying to calm her down.

"He brought me flowers every week." She seemed to calm down and think. "If he forgot to say 'I love you', he would apologize. He never forgot to kiss me every day."

"Sounds like me and my wife." Jacob smiled to himself.

"You sound like a lucky man." He could almost feel her smile which sent a sense of warmth within him.

"Until a year ago, I was." Jacob stared at the ground.

"I'm sorry. Do you miss her?" She seemed to take a deep breath.

"Every day." The tears welled up as he thought about Helen, his wife.

"That's a good thing." She stood up and began to walk into the forest.

"Where are you going?" Jacob was concerned about her safety. "Who are you?"

"I have to leave, the dawn is here." She sniffled a few times. "I have to be elsewhere."

"Will I see you again?" Jacob tried to follow her.

"No." The sorrow in her voice was so very overwhelming.

The sun started to filter through the trees as she let down her hood and turned to look at him.

"Helen?" Jacob cried out moving toward her, but the sun blinded him.

As he rubbed his eyes and searched the forest, she was gone. Looking through the forest, there was no trace of the woman he thought was his wife.

The Willows

The legend of the Willows went back two centuries with the account of two lovers who ran away from their families into the grove of willows. Since then every ten years another couple disappeared without a trace.

Sometimes, passersby would hear whispering or faint laughter. Some tried to enter the grove to see if anything or anyone was there, but only found themselves at a clearing on the other side.

Ann and Jim had been secretly dating for a year. They knew their parents would not approve, but they were in love.

"So many escaped through the grove." Ann pleaded. "Why couldn't we?"

"Remember Fred and Laura who went in and never came back?" Jim wasn't sure it would be the answer they were looking for.

"Let's go in." Ann wanted to get away.

"So many have disappeared into the grove and never came back." Jim hesitated thinking as many bad things as good could happen.

"But it's romantic." Ann pulled him toward the grove.

"We don't know what really happened to those who disappeared." Jim stood his ground.

"Don't be a baby." Ann teased him. "I'll bet they are happy and free. We can even date in the open."

"I'd rather stay here." Jim insisted.

"Come on, Jim." Ann pulled him into the willows.

As they passed by the first row of willows, a vast field or reeds greeted them.

"I never knew this was here!" Jim looked around in awe.

"Over there!" Ann pointed to huge mansion on a far hill.

"We don't know who lives there." Jim wanted to go back.

"Then let's find out!" Ann ran ahead of him letting the excitement overwhelm her.

"Ann! Wait!" Jim ran after her.

As he slowly fell behind her, Jim started just walk toward the mansion. He watched as Ann knocked on the door which opened letting her in.

When Jim knocked on the door, a gruff voice grumbled "Go away!"

"Let me in!" Jim worried about Ann. "Ann!"

No answer came so Jim decided to look in the windows, but what he saw froze him in place. Some great ugly creature held Ann in its grasp. She had fainted seeing the monster close to her face.

"No!" Jim watched in horror as the creature placed Ann into a cage with four others. The ogre turned towards Jim and sneered.

"Go away!" The creature waved Jim away.

Jim heard the patter of snarling animals coming from behind the mansion. He started to run back through the reeds as two snarling emaciated wolves coming towards him.

Jim ran through the field hoping he could escape the snapping jaws. Spoon he came to the point where he and Ann entered. A dark space was in front of him as he jumped into the darkness finding himself outside the grove.

"Jim?" An elderly man was standing over him.

"Help me?" Jim pleaded, hating himself for running away.

"What's wrong?" the old man was confused.

"My girl friend is captive in a mansion on the other side of the willows." Jim wanted to go back.

"Mine, too." The old man reached down and helped Jim up.

"You've been there, too?" Jim looked hard at the old man, but didn't recognize him.

"My name is Fred." The old man tried to smile. "I've been waiting for you for the past fifty years."

"Fifty years!" Jim looked around seeing so many changes that happened to the town.

"I came back young, too, until I realized I stayed too long on the other side." Fred sighed. "I was told you and Ann disappeared and have been coming here every month waiting for you."

"I have to go back to save her!" Jim looked back, but the darkness had gone.

"It's too late." Fred knew what he was looking for. "Your time has passed. At least, you survived like I did."

"What's happened to Ann?" Jim started to cry.

"It's been fifty years, Jim." Fred tried to console him. "They're both gone, my love and yours."

"How come I haven't aged?" Jim looked at Fred and then himself.

"I don't know." Fred put his arm around Jim and walked him away down the street.

Night Calls

Linda and Ruth held hands whenever they passed Karen's cabin in the forest. It was a quiet path that brought them to their houses quicker after school. They were nervous passing this place because they were told Karen was a witch and dangerous.

Going around would force them to encounter the Johnson twins who would terrorize them all the way home. It. also, meant an extra 30 minutes of walking home.

Linda and Ruth both had heard how local hunters encountered Karen while they were stalking deer. Odd night calls would scare the deer before the hunters could get a shot off. Afterwards, they heard Karen cackling from inside her cabin.

No one had seen her, but knew she lived there. One night, two hunters decided to confront her and entered her cabin. They looked around, but did not find her home.

As they left, they heard Karen laughing at them, but what terrified them was the growling of some creature that thrashed its way towards them through the tall grass.

A chill ran up their spines as some invisible force crashed through the undergrowth toward them. It forced them to run away without seeing what it was. When the reached the edge of the forest, whatever it was became silent.

It was a Friday with the sun setting which Linda and Ruth knew staying after school would make it harder to get home before dark. They quicken their pace until they reached Karen's cabin.

"Hurry Linda!" Ruth saw that she had slowed down to look at the cabin.

"I'm trying!" Linda did not want to rush since she was having a trouble carrying her books.

"I hope she's not home." Ruth looked anxiously looked over at the cabin. They had never seen Karen. only heard what the hunters told them. The hunters insisted she had to be old, ugly and dangerous though they never met her.

A light went on inside the cabin and the front door opened. Ruth and Linda stopped dead in their tracks staring at the open door.

"Don't look!" Ruth had the idea they would turn to stone if they saw her.

"Children?" A beautiful young woman stood in the doorway.

"Is that you, Karen?" Linda was agog at seeing her.

"I've seen you girls walk by here every day and hurry past my home." Karen stood still.

"We were told you were a witch." Linda

hesitated, but soon relaxed. How could someone so beautiful be a witch?

"Do I look like a witch?" Karen smiled at them.

"No." Linda quickly answered.

"I've never seen a witch." Ruth hesitated. "We don't know you."

"Then come in and I'll make you some ice tea." Karen beckoned them over.

"I don't know." Ruth fought the urge to run.

"It looks safe." Linda wanted to see inside.

"We have to go home." Ruth refused to go in and tried to pull Linda away.

"Then I'll let you know." Linda shook Ruth off and entered the cabin.

"How about you?" Karen offered her hand to Ruth who was afraid.

"Linda come back!" Ruth cried out suddenly as Karen started to close the door changing into a hideous old woman she really was.

The sound of some snarling beast thrashed its way toward Ruth. She started to run dropping her books as she went. The sound of whatever followed soon faded away as she came closer home.

Ruth's parents called the police who stopped by Linda's house to pick up her parents. They all marched down to Karen's cabin. When they got there, all they found was a ruined structure that never seemed to survive a massive fire.

No one could have possibly lived in the ruins. Ruth insisted that her friend entered the cabin and Karen was with her. The police restrained Ruth from going into the crumbled cabin.

A search was made for Linda, but she was never found. To this day, hunters came upon the cabin and found it in one piece. They told others that they were certain two people lived there now. However , when the police came to investigate only the charred remains of the cabin lay in ruins.

Ruth came by only once and found the cabin

intact. Standing in front of the window, Ruth saw two old women staring back at her. The smaller of the two waved to Ruth which sent a chill down her spine.

Ruth heard the snarling again of some creature that chased her out of the forest. She cried knowing she would never see Linda again. Ruth decided that she would never look for her and was thankful she didn't follow Linda into the cabin.

The Maze

"This will be great!" George told his friends ay the grand opening of his rock and garden maze. All of them were surprised George invited them since the last fiasco party he held last month.

The maze was an acre wide with paths and dead ends. There were large trees that the maze encircled. Each tree had faces which had smiles, frowns or surprised looks.

His friends all said privately that they would never attend one of George's parties, but he insisted that they all come one more time.

"I thought this might work out better than the last time." George looked into the five faces that weren't so sure they should stay. "The first one to make it out of the maze will win fifty dollars."

"Only fifty?" Laura thought it pretty cheap. "How long will we have to get out?"

"Well, Laura, I know how impatient you are so I'll come get you if you get bored." George thought he might let her suffer a while before he came. "However, there are traps and surprises all over the maze. There are a couple of gifts that could help through the maze. I don't want you to hurt yourselves so be careful."

"That doesn't sound like fun." Gilbert, a rather rotund individual didn't want to spend too much time in the maze either.

"All right." George sighed. "How about five hundred dollars to the one gets who out of the maze first."

"That's better." Gilbert wiped the sweat from his forehead though it was the beginning of Fall.

"Anyone else?" George saw little else that would stop the game.

"When do we start?" Sandra, a short dowdy girl of twenty was anxious to get it over with.

"Now if you like, but one at a time." George stood at the opening.

"Why one at a time?" John, who stood behind them all asked.

"That way, you won't bunch up in one place." George tired of this game. "As you enter, the walls will shift into a different part of the maze."

"That's not fair!" Gilbert protested.

"No one who goes in last will be at a certain disadvantage which is why within the maze will change." George hoped that he didn't convince them all not to go in.

"How do we know you didn't rig the maze?" Joyce never trusted George, but she did like these type of games. Besides, she could use five hundred dollars.

"I just told you I did." George smiled at her. "It'll be fun I promise you."

"I'll go first." Tony kept quiet enough and the sooner he went in, the sooner he could get the chance at five hundred dollars.

"Okay! Listen!" The all started to talk at once. "After all of you have gone in, I'll be waiting for you on the other side."

"Where's the end?" Laura thought George might tell them.

"Wherever the end happens to be." George pointed in two directions.

"Can we start?" Tony wanted to get started.

"Come on, Tony." George him into the maze and immediately a wall of vines rose behind Tony.

"Joyce?" George led her down a different path within the maze and another wall of vines closed behind her.

Soon all five were in the maze separated by green ivied walls over ten feet high. George heard mumbling which he enjoyed no end as he walked around the south side of the maze. He would've been surprised if someone did eventually come out.

What George didn't tell them was that the faces on the trees were masks from Peru and Ecuador which held curses and poison darts that shot from their eyes.

There were pits with sharp sticks pointing upward and a pond with Water Moccasins around the perimeter. Another thing he didn't tell them was that he hated them all for ruining his party only 6 months ago. It cost him his job, but he had enough money to survive.

"George! I've had enough!" Joyce was the first to give up. "I'm lost!"

She heard no answer and called out to the others. No one answered. One more turn took her to a great oak with a creepy mask attached to the trunk. She almost heard a snarl coming out of the angry face as she tried to pass by.

"This isn't funny." Joyce thought she saw a closed-circuit TV camera behind the eyes. As she backed away, a sharp pain pierced her spine. Blood trickled down her mouth and as she looked down saw the trip wire that launched a poisoned dart into her back.

Tony was getting frustrated at the random moving of the walls of ivy. At times he picked up a stray branch and beat the walls. Eventually, an ivied wall opened up to a small pond. There was a fountain near the edge and Tony was thirsty.

"This is not worth it." Tony leaned over and tasted the water. It was cool spring water which he gulped down.

He felt something wrap around his leg. Startled he found a Water Moccasin raise its head to strike. Too late Tony tried to shake it off, but he felt not one bite yet others as he fell back into the pond. Soon he felt paralyzed and unable to breath.

One by one the others succumbed to a painful death. George waited long enough to be sure no one survived the maze. The masks he bought were truly cursed and now he got the revenge he prayed for.

To be sure. George called out all their names with no answers. He decided to go in and make sure which brought a smile to his face. As he entered, a wall of ivy closed behind him. George was not concerned until a second and third wall closed behind him. After a few hours, George realized he was lost in the maze.

Locals

"I've never seen this town before." Linda wondered as she and her husband, Jim, took a short cut home. It was supposed to cut an hour off their trip.

"It's the first time we took this route." Jim reminded her. What interested in him was that there were no cars on the street or people walking about.

"Everything looks different with half the town boarded up." Linda worried that they were in real trouble.

"There's a few people!" Jim thought he saw a few people entering stores, but he thought they were dressed in rags. It happened so fast, he wasn't sure.

"I don't like this." Linda took a deep breath.

"Keep driving, Lin." Jim wanted to get out fast.

"We have to know if we're lost." Linda looked for someone to ask directions. "Let's ask someone."

"There are a couple of locals, but they seem too local." Jim pointed to a man and woman standing and staring at him.

"Hello?" Linda pulled over and rolled down her window.

The man and woman walked up to her with a smile, but there was a sadness behind the smile. Jim sat and stared at them

"Hi! I'm Chet and this is my wife Carol."

Chet was in his early thirties wearing jeans and a polo shirt. Carol was in a plaid dress which was not very flattering.

"What can we do for you?" Carol leaned over, a tear visible below her left eye.

"We're trying to get to Hanover, but we seemed to be lost." Linda almost asked why Carol was crying, but it was none of her business.

"You might try driving straight down the road there out of town." Chet pointed ahead of them. "I hope you find the entrance to the interstate which is just a couple miles away."

"Thanks!" Jim heard enough. "Let's get out of here!"

"Well, thank you." Linda rolled up her window and then turned to him. "You don't have to be rude!"

"Lin…" Jim hesitated looking up and down the town as they left. "Did you notice that we are the only car on the street? No trucks?"

"Does it matter?" Linda started down the road leading out of town.

They drove a couple of miles, but didn't see any entrance to the interstate. A mile further they found themselves at the edge of another town.

"Now where are we?" Jim was impatient.

"Let's ask them over the…." Linda saw the same couple waiting for them on the side of the road.

"We've been going around in circles!" Jim wanted to slap the smiles off these people.

"HI, again." Linda tried to make the best of it.

"Hi, I'm Chet and this is my wife Carol." Chet had the same sad smile and acted if they hadn't met before. Carol wiped a tear from her eye, but continued to smile.

"What can we do for you?" Carol leaned

over to Linda's window.

"How about telling us how to get out of this town?" Jim called out across from Linda.

"The only way out is down this road." Chet patiently pointed ahead of them.

"We didn't see an entrance to the interstate and this road leads us back to here." Linda couldn't hide her frustration.

"It's the only way we know." Carol sobbed and turned away.

"Are you all right?" Linda felt sorry for her.

"She's upset since now we are leaving this place." Chet was not happy either.

"So, you know how to get out of here?" Jim started to get sarcastic.

"Yes, sadly, only one way." Chet winced as he held his wife's hand.

"Well, we'll try it again." Linda shook her head and started out of town.

A few miles later, Linda and Jim found themselves in the same town. They looked at each other before Linda tried to slow down.

"Oh no! Floor it! Get out of here!" Jim put his foot on Linda's to push the care ahead. As they came closer to Chet and Carol, the couple walked in front of the car. It was the last thing Linda and Jim remembered.

Warren and Julie found themselves lost on a road they thought would save themselves, at least, an hour of driving. When a town presented itself, they sighed a sigh of relief.

"There's someone over there." Warren pointed at a couple standing in front of a hardware store.

"Hello?" Julie rolled down her window as

the couple walked up to them. She noticed the woman had been crying.

"Hi! I'm Jim and this is my wife Linda." Jim was wearing jeans and a polo shirt while Linda wore a plaid dress.

"What can we do for you?" Linda leaned over with a tear in her left eye.

"I think we're lost." Warren already wanted to leave this town.

Better Off Dead

"Everyone ready to go outside?" Melanie cheerfully gave out glasses that they were told was to shield their eyes from low radiation and bright sunlight.

"Why do we need glasses?" Henry, a young child, asked his mom.

"Too many have gone blind by not using them." His mom, Frieda, patted him on the head.

"Remember, only go within the signs around the park and be back in two hours." Melanie cautioned them and then waved them through the outside doors.

"Why can't we just go outside?" Henry hated wearing these glasses that strapped around his head. The last time he tripped over a log that was bigger than he was.

"It wouldn't be safe." Frieda gently pushed him outside.

"I don't want to stay inside anymore." Henry tried to take his glasses off, but the strap was too tight.

"Behave Henry!" Frieda slapped his hand away.

The great iron doors of the enclosure compound began to open. Fourteen travelers ventured out. What they saw was the same lush green horizon as always. The skies were blue and the sun even bright with the glasses on.

"If only the war ended sooner." Jake Anderson seemed to say the same thing every time he was let out. "We could have enjoyed this without protection."

"I remember." Frieda agreed.

"What are we missing?" Harold Pinkton was tired of getting only two hours of freedom a month.

"What can we do?" Frieda was just as frustrated, but was glad for even the two hours.

"Why don't we take the glasses off?" Henry chimed up. "They can't punish all of us."

"Would rather never to go outside again?" Frieda knew it wasn't' possible.

"If we did take the glasses off the light or the radiation would blind us." Jake thought they were wasting time.

"What if they're lying?" Henry tripped over a log. He reached down to find something soft and squishy.

"Henry? What's the matter?" Frieda saw the funny look on his face.

"The log is soft." Henry picked up pieces of bark.

"It's just a log." Harold picked Henry up.

"Something that always bothered me." Leonard Stimpkins touched his glasses. "I remember seeing this before."

"How so?" Harold looked around thinking something was wrong.

"There's a squirrel that's always on the same tree when we get this far." Leonard stared at it. "If I'm right, that squirrel will jump to that tree then come down and run in that direction."

As they watched, the squirrel did exactly what he said. Then Henry chimed up.

"Then maybe the same birds will fly over our heads about now." Henry pointed skyward as a flock of birds fly over them.

"It must be the glasses!" Leonard tried to undo the straps on his glasses.

"Let me." Frieda turned him around. She wondered what was going on.

"I've got a knife." Leonard took out one from his pocket.

"That's not allowed!" Harold wanted no part of it and walked away with the others.

"Hold still!" Frieda cut through the straps.

"Oh, no!" Leonard removed his glasses.

"Me next!" Henry pulled on his glasses.

"What's the matter, Len?" Frieda worried about his reaction.

"Keep your glasses on!" Leonard tried to put his glasses back on, but they crumbled in his hands.

"Why? What do you see?" Frieda put the

knife away.

"Go back." Leonard started to cry.

"Tell me!" Frieda whispered harshly.

"There's nothing left and your son is standing next to a dead body...not a log." Leonard whispered back.

Leonard's face and voice started to fade away. Frieda began to feel very afraid.

"Desolation! Rose colored glasses!" Leonard could be heard faintly.

"Henry! We have to go back." Frieda looked for Henry and noticed that no one else was around them.

"Where did everybody go, momma?" Henry took her hand.

"We have to go back!" Frieda hurried Henry back to the front door of the huge concrete complex they had called home.

Frieda hadn't noticed that the building was totally of concrete. It was of fine oak and steel every other time. Then she noticed her glasses were cracked.

"Let us in!" Henry banged on the door unaware of his surroundings.

"You're too late." A mechanical voice answered him.

"Let us in!" Frieda expected to hear Melanie's voice not this one.

"Melanie, let us in!" Henry distinctly heard her voice though Frieda didn't.

Frieda looked down and saw the blood on Henry's hands and pants. She looked back for Leonard, but he was nowhere in sight,

"Please, let my son in!" Frieda was frightened.

"Stand back!" the voice urged her backward a few feet.

The doors opened a crack to let Henry in.

Frieda cried as Henry looked back, but he saw his mom smiling and waving to him.

"See you soon." Henry heard his mom say though her mouth was shut from grief.

"No, we won't." Leonard stood next to Frieda. "We know the truth now. They'll never let us back in."

"What's going on?" Frieda took out the knife and cut off the strap to her glasses and saw what Leonard saw.

"The rest of the world is gone." Leonard tried to understand. "We were given those glasses to convince us there was hope. Yet, out there, there is no hope."

"What'll happen to us?" Frieda stared at the locked door of the concrete prison she thought was home.

"We can't be out here much longer." Leonard saw the dead bodies lying around the walls that seemed to extend a mile.

"Where do we go?" Frieda's tears were flowing now.

"They used the glasses to continue a lie with virtual reality." Leonard didn't know what to do either.

"Nothing was real." Frieda wanted to bang on the door and promise not to tell anyone. She searched the devastation without an escape.

"Only this." Leonard spread his arms wide in surrender. "We're better off dead."

Made in the USA
Columbia, SC
27 January 2018